Contents Cloudbabies

Introduction	06
Baba Pink	08
Baba Yellow	09
Baba Blue	10
Baba Green	11
The Cloudbabies' Friends	12
The Cloudbabies' Favourite things	14
All About Spring	16
Baba Green's Spring Flower	17
Mystery Journey	18
Green Fingers	19
What are Clouds and What is Rain?	20
What is a Rainbow?	21
Colouring In	22
Spot the Cloudy Difference	23
Hide and Seek	24
Has Anyone Seen Sun?	26
All About Summer	38
Baba Yellow's Fan	39
Colouring In	40
What is the Sun?	42
What is Day?	43
Match the Pairs	44
Lost Skydonk	45
Colouring In	46
Cloudbabies String Painting	47
Mystery Noise	48
All About Autumn	60
Baba Blue's Leaf Rubbing	61
Odd One Out	62
Sky Words	63
Fuffa's Make and Do	64
Counting	66
Memory Game	67
What is Wind?	68
Make a Windsock	69
Snowbaby	70
All About Winter	82
Baba Pink's Sparkly Pinecones	83
Sky Friends	84
Star Eve Bunting	85
What is Night?	86
What is the Moon?	87
Colouring In	88
Colouring In	89
Night Sky Biscuits	90
Colouring In	91
Starry Night	92
Answers	93

£7.99

Published 2013. Century Books Ltd.
Unit 1, Upside Station Building Solsbro Road,
Torquay, Devon, UK, TQ26FD

who looks after the sky?
the Cloudbabies® do!

Hello and welcome to the Cloudbabies' very first annual!

Baba Pink, Baba Blue, Baba Yellow and Baba Green can't wait for you to join in with their games and puzzles.

There are lots of fun stories to enjoy too!

The Cloudbabies love doing their jobs. Every day they jump on their Skyhorsies and set off to take care of their Sky Friends.

✳ Polishing Sun!
✳ Painting Rainbow!
✳ Fluffing up the clouds!

You can help to take care of the sky too. Start by looking for ten Little Stars that are playing hide and seek in the pages of this annual. When you find one, write down the page number where it's hiding.

Who polishes the Sun?
Cloudbabies!
Wipes the cobwebs from the Moon?
Cloudbabies!
Who tells the bedtime stories to the stars?
Cloudbabies! Cloudbabies!
Who paints the colours on the Rainbow and makes everything look new?
Who looks after the sky?
The Cloudbabies do!

babapink

Favourite colour: **pink**

Favourite shape: **star** ⭐

Baba Pink loves caring for her friends.
She carries a handbag filled with 'mummy
stuff' to clean, stitch and mend. Her
favourite thing is her feather duster.

She likes to look after the others,
and can be bossy at times!
But everyone loves her
caring nature.

Baba Pink's Favourite Things

Caring
kit

Polishing
Sun!

Feather
duster

babayellow

Favourite colour: yellow

Favourite shape: sun

Baba Yellow is quiet and shy, but she is also very artistic. Her satchel is filled with paints and brushes.

Her favourite thing is her Fluteytoot, and everyone loves to listen to her play. She is a little bit forgetful, but very sunny and bright.

Baba Yellow's Favourite Things

Fluteytoot

Satchel

Painting Rainbow's stripes

baba blue

Favourite colour: blue

Favourite shape: moon

Baba Blue is very good at mending and fixing things that are broken. But sometimes he is a little bit clumsy!

He loves doing his jobs and playing with the other Cloudbabies. His favourite thing is his toolbox, which is filled with lots of useful things and he can always find a way to help a friend in need.

Baba Blue's Favourite Things

Hammer

Toolbox

Star flinging

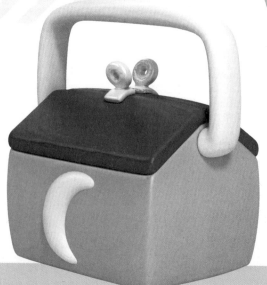

babagreen

Favourite colour: green

Favourite shape: cloud

Baba Green is quiet and thoughtful. He loves working in the garden, looking after the plants and flowers.

Baba Green enjoys making up stories for his friends and they love listening to them!

Baba Green's Favourite Things

Spade

Planting and growing his beanie beans

Watering can

Bobo White

This sweet little Sky Imp lives with the Cloudbabies. They found him asleep at the bottom of the Rainbow. He is full of fun and a little bit mischievous! He rides around on Skydonk and dreams of becoming a proper Cloudbaby one day.

Little Star

Little Star is very young and he loves learning about the Sky World around him. It is his job to twinkle at night, so he has to sleep all day long. But he is so curious about everything that he sometimes jumps out of his bed too early!

Fuffa Cloud

Fuffa Cloud is a little cloud who is learning how to rain, with the help of the Cloudbabies of course! She loves playing tricks on the others. The Cloudbabies fluff her up every day but she doesn't like it very much!

Rainbow

Rainbow is proud of his bright colours and he loves showing them off! He can be a little bit grumpy but he has a very kind heart. He helps Baba Blue to fling the stars into the night sky.

Sun

Big and friendly Sun loves to laugh! He's very jolly and can always cheer his friends up if they are feeling sad. Sun loves to look clean and shiny, so he especially enjoys being polished by Baba Pink.

Moon

Moon is shy, gentle and caring. The Cloudbabies dust and polish her so she always looks her best. She eats moonrock to help her turn into a beautiful full moon.

The Cloudyhouse

The Cloudbabies live in in a wonderful, colourful house. It has lots of different shaped windows, and the rooms are shaped just like clouds.

Startree

The Startree is where the shooting stars grow. Every evening the Cloudbabies pick the stars from the Startree and fling them into the night sky.

Skyhorsies

When the Cloudbabies need to get up, up into the sky to do their jobs, they jump on their Skyhorsies. The Skyhorsies eat horseyhay, but sometimes they have rainpears as a special treat.

Greenhorsey

Bluehorsey

Yellowhorsey

Pinkhorsey

Skytrain

The Skytrain is made out of clouds and helps the Cloudbabies to get around the sky. Sometimes they use it to carry stars and moonrock. Sometimes they go in search of missing snow clouds. But sometimes the Cloudbabies just want to go for a train ride!

Skydonk   Rainpears

Colourful Skydonk carries Bobo White wherever he wants to go. He is a little bit shy, but he loves spending time with Bobo White. They have a lot of fun together!

Delicious rainpears grow in the Sky Orchard. The Cloudbabies eat them as snacks and sometimes they give them to the Skyhorsies. The Cloudbabies love using them to make rainpear juice and rainpear pies too!

All About Spring

Spring is the first season of the year. It is warmer than winter, and there are more hours of sunlight in the day. Some spring days are sunny and hot.

Spring is Baba Green's favourite time of year!

What is a Season?

A season is a time of year. The year is split up into four seasons and each one has different weather.

Signs of Spring

Clouds rain and help the plants grow.

✿ Flowers burst into bloom.

✿ Trees grow new leaves.

✿ Baby lambs are born.

✿ You can hear lots of birdsong.

Baba Green's Spring Flower

make & do

You will need

- Paper plate
- Green poster paint

  Paintbrush
- Glue
- Pink, white and yellow construction paper
- Scissors

  Pencil
- Glitter in your favourite colours

 Always ask a grown-up to help you when using scissors.

your petal template

Make a beautiful paper plate flower with Baba Green.

1. Paint your plate all over with green paint and wait for it to dry.

2. Use a pencil to trace the petal shapes onto pink and white construction paper.

3. Ask your grown-up to help you cut out the petals.

4. Turn the plate over so that you can decorate the bottom of it.

5. Stick the petals around the edge of the plate with glue.

6. Ask your grown-up to help you cut a circle out of yellow construction paper.

7. Glue the circle onto the centre of the plate.

8. Finish your flower with colourful glitter!

Spring Fun

❀ When it's sunny, go on a nature walk.

❀ When it's raining, put on your wellies and jump in some puddles.

❀ In the garden, plant flowers that bees and butterflies will love.

Mystery Journey

What is Baba Blue
travelling around in?

Join the dots to find out.

Green Fingers

You will need

- Clean, empty yoghurt pots
- Bean seeds
- Multi-use compost
- Bamboo canes
- String
- A patch of garden
- A grown-up to help you

At the end of April, Baba Green starts growing beanie beans. Yummy! Why don't you try growing some runner beans?

1. Ask your grown-up to help you make some small draining holes in the bottom of the yoghurt pots.

2. Count out a bean seed for each pot.

3. Fill each pot with compost.

4. In the first pot, make a hole in the compost with your finger, about 4cm deep. Place a bean seed in the hole. Then cover it with compost. Repeat this for each pot.

5. Put each pot on a saucer and water it.

6. Put the pots in a cool, dry place, away from bright sunshine. Keep them watered so the compost doesn't get dry.

7. When the shoots are about 5cm high, it is time to plant them in the ground. In your patch of garden, ask your grown-up to help you make a wigwam shape with the bamboo canes and string.

8. Dig a hole on each side of every cane. Put a plant in each hole and water them.

9. It is important to keep the plants well watered.

10. Wait for the beans to grow and then pick and eat them!

Did You Know...?

In spring, the clouds send lots of rain to water the plants and flowers.

What are Clouds?

When the air is hot and dry, it soaks up water from ponds, puddles and streams. The water gets turned into clouds!

Clouds are like steam from a kettle. They are made of tiny drops of water.

The water drops are so small and light that they can float in the air.

When the water drops gather together, they make clouds in the sky!

What is Rain?

Rain is made when clouds turn into water again.

The clouds get heavier and heavier.

Warm air holds more water than cool air.

When the air gets cooler, the heavy clouds have to let go of some water.

The water falls out of the sky as rain!

What is a Rainbow?

Did You Know?

Did you know that sunlight is made of seven colours?

To see a rainbow, you have to be standing between the sun and the rain.

Red **Orange** **Yellow** **Green** **Blue** **Indigo** **Violet**

Usually you can't see all the colours. But when it is sunny and rainy at the same time, something special happens.

The sunlight shines through the raindrops.

The water bends the sunlight so that you can see the colours.

That's what makes a rainbow!

What do you wear when it rains? Colour in this big umbrella, and draw a picture of yourself holding it.

Ready for Fun?

Colour in all four happy Cloudbabies!

Spot the Cloudy Difference?

The Cloudbabies love their Cloudyhouse. There are five differences between these pictures. Can you spot them all?

Hide and Seek

Fuffa Cloud is playing hide and seek with the Cloudbabies. Can you spot everyone in the picture? Put a tick in the box for everyone you find.

24

Has Anyone Seen Sun?

High in the sky, up, up, in the clouds ...

The Cloud Babies are playing hide and seek. "Coming! Ready or not!" calls Baba Green.

Sun wants to know what the Cloudbabies are doing. It looks like a lot of fun!

Baba Green spots Baba Blue and Baba Yellow behind a cloud. "Found you!" he calls. Baba Blue and Baba Yellow giggle.

"Hello, Baba Green," says Sun. "Are you playing hide and seek?" "Yes, Sun," says Baba Green. "And I'm going to find everyone."

Baba Green finds Baba Pink behind another cloud.
"Have I won?" asks Baba Pink.
"No," says Baba Yellow. "Bobo White's still hiding."

Sun thinks the game is very exciting. Then they hear Skydonk's voice. "Hee-haw!"

Skydonk's voice is coming from the horseyhay field. "Found you!" says Baba Green. "Bobo win!" says Bobo White.

"Well done, Bobo White!" says Baba Blue. "Let's play again!"
Sun bounces up and down.

"Can I play this time?" he asks.
"Hide and seek might be a bit too difficult for you, Sun," says Baba Pink. "You are VERY big and VERY bright."

But Sun really wants to play. So the Cloudbabies let him join in.
"My turn to count," says Baba Yellow.
"One, two, three, four, five . . ."
Sun looks around. Where can he hide?

Sun slips behind a little cloud. Perfect!
"Coming! Ready or not!" calls Baba Yellow.

She spots Sun straight away. "Found you, Sun!" she says.

"Ohhh!" says Sun in a sad voice. "Can I have another go?"
The other Cloudbabies come out of their hiding places.
"Maybe you just need some practice," says Baba Green.

Sun tries lots of different hiding places.

The Cloudyhouse

The Star Tree   Even some horseyhay!

But nothing works. Sun is fed up.

"I'm just no good at hiding," he says with a big sigh.
"Maybe we should play a different game," says Baba Blue.
"But I LIKE hide and seek!" says Sun.

The Cloudbabies don't have time to play any more games. They have to go and do their jobs.
"Sorry, Sun," says Baba Yellow. "Maybe we can play again tomorrow."

The Cloudbabies hurry off to do their jobs. But Sun is still thinking about hide and seek. "If only I could just find ONE good hiding place . . ." he says.

Then he spots Bobo White playing hide and seek with Skydonk.
Skydonk is trying to hide behind some horseyhay.

"Skydonk needs to find a bigger hiding place than that," says Sun with a chuckle Then he has a wonderful idea. "That's what I need!" he says, " A bigger hiding place!"

Meanwhile Baba Pink is busy fluffing up the clouds. Fuffa Cloud tries to sneak away. She doesn't like being fluffed!

Baba Yellow is painting Rainbow. Suddenly, the sky starts to turn dark blue.
"Nighting time already?" gasps Baba Yellow.

Baba Green is watering his seedlings.

He looks up in surprise and waters his own feet by mistake.

Baba Blue is picking stars from the Startree.
"Nighting time?" he says. "But I've only just started picking shooting stars."

Fuffa Cloud doesn't want to go to bed.
"I'm sorry, Fuffa, says Baba Pink. "Nighting time does seem to have happened rather quickly today."

"But I'm not tired!" Fuffa Cloud complains.

Little Star gets out of bed. He looks very sleepy. "Nighting time?" he says, yawning. "OK! Little Star will twinkle now."

"Fuffa Cloud's not tired, but Little Star looks VERY sleepy," says Baba Pink. "There's something funny about this nighting time."

The Cloudbabies don't feel ready for bed.
"Do you think it really IS nighting time?" asks Baba Green.
"It must be," says Baba Blue. "Sun's gone to bed."

"Maybe Sun's gone to bed too early," says Baba Pink.
"Why would he do that?" asks Baba Green.

The Cloudbabies decide to ask Sun why he has gone to bed.

They ride up to Sun's Cloudybed. But they get a big surprise.

The cloud is empty!

"Sun's not in his bed!" cries Baba Pink.
"What if he doesn't come back?"

Just then, Moon floats up beside
them and yawns.

"Don't worry, Baba Pink," she says. "Sun says if you can find him, he'll come back."

Sun is still playing hide and seek!

"So, do you think you can find him?" asks Moon.
"Oh yes!" the Cloudbabies cry.
"Coming, Sun!" calls Baba Blue.
"Ready or not!"

The Cloudbabies look everywhere for Sun.

The Cloudyhouse

The Sky Stables   The Star Tree

Even under the
horseyhay!

Sun is nowhere to be seen.
"We've looked everywhere," Baba Blue tells
Moon. "But we just can't find him."

Moon smiles.
"You all give up?" she asks.
The Cloudbabies and Bobo
White nod.
Then they hear a friendly
chuckle.

Sun is hiding behind Moon!
"Da-Da!" says Sun. "Did you like
my hiding place?"

"Sun is best!" says Bobo White.

Sun is very happy, and the sky
is blue again.
"Hey, Rainbow!" calls Baba
Yellow. "Time for that repaint!"

"Shooting stars to pick," says Baba Blue.
"And seedlings to water," says Baba Green.

"Sun, it's soooo nice to have you back!" says Baba Pink. She gives him a big hug.

Moon yawns and floats back to her bed.
"I've got some sleep to catch up on," she says.

Now that Sun is out of his hiding place, everything can go back to normal ...

As long as someone tells Little Star where nighting time has gone!

All About Summer

Summer is the second season of the year. It is the warmest season. It has the most hours of sunlight and the smallest amount of rain.

What is Temperature?

Temperature is how hot or cold something is. You can measure temperature with a thermometer.

Signs of Summer

* The sky is very blue.
* The sun is very hot.
* Gardens are filled with flowers.
* Tasty vegetables and fruit grow in the fields.
* Lots of families go on holiday.

Baba Yellow's Fan

make & do

Baba Yellow's handy fan will keep you cool on a hot summer day.

You will need

- A roll of paper that's about 100 x 20cm wide
- Scissors
- Two wide lolly sticks
- Glue
- Sticky tape
- Crayons, pencils or stickers

⚠ Always ask a grown-up to help you when using scissors.

1 Ask your grown-up to help you cut a long piece of paper from the roll.

2 Use your crayons, pencils or stickers to decorate the fan on both sides.

3 Fold the paper into pleats, like a concertina. The pleats should be the same width as the lolly sticks.

4 Glue a lolly stick to each end of the folded paper. The sticks should poke out over the top of the paper by about 2cm, so that part of the folded paper is uncovered at the bottom.

5 Press the pleats together and carefully bind sticky tape around the uncovered paper at the bottom of the fan.

6 To open your fan, bring the lolly sticks all the way round so that they meet!

Summer Fun

- Splash in a paddling pool in your garden.
- Visit a beach and explore the rockpools.
- Use old cardboard boxes to build dens outside.

Favourite Things

The word 'summer' begins with the letter 's'.
What else begins with the same letter?
Colour in everything that starts with the letter 's'.

Sun's Sunset

Sun wants to see a sunset!
Colour in this evening
picture for him.

Did YOU Know...?

In summer, the days are long and the sun shines brightly.

✳ The solar system is very, very big.

✳ It is made up of the sun and everything that travels around it.

✳ You live on a planet called Earth.

✳ Earth is part of the solar system.

✳ The sun, the moon and all the stars in the sky are part of the solar system too.

What is the Sun?

✳ The sun is a very big, very special kind of star.

✳ It is in the centre of the solar system.

✳ It makes its own light and heat.

✳ The heat travels out from the sun and warms the Earth.

✳ The sun is the biggest thing in our solar system!

What is Day?

✳ The Earth spins around the sun.

✳ When the place where you live is pointing towards the bright sun, it is daytime.

You might take these things to the beach on a sunny day. Can you name them all?

Draw lines to match up the
pairs and say what they are.

Lost Skydonk

Bobo White wants to play, but he can't find Skydonk anywhere. Can you help him to look for his friend?

Colour in Bobo White and Skydonk.
Use the picture to help you.

Cloudbabies String Painting

You will need

- **Thick paper or thin card.**
- **Scissors**
- **Ball of thick string**
- **4 saucers**
- **Heavy Book**
- **Green, yellow, pink and blue paint**

⚠️ Always ask a grown-up to help you when using scissors.

Have you ever tried painting with string? Let Baba Yellow show you how!

1 Fold a piece of paper in half, like a birthday card.

2 Ask your grown-up to help you cut four lengths of string. Each one should be longer than the piece of paper.

3 Tip a different paint colour into each of the four saucers.

4 Dip the first piece of string in the yellow paint.

5 Open the folded paper and lay the string in a twirly pattern on the right-hand side. Leave one end of the string sticking out over the edge of paper.

6 Repeat steps 4 to 5 for each colour.

7 Fold the other half of the paper down over the string and place a heavy book on top.

8 Take the ends of the string and pull out the pieces one by one.

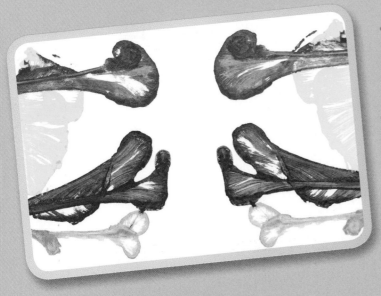

Mystery Noise

High in the sky, up, up, in the clouds ...

It's nearly time for bed. Baba Pink is giving Sun his bedtime bath.

Baba Pink wipes the soapy water away.
"There, all done," she says.
"Oh thank you, Baba Pink," says Sun.

He gives a BIG yawn.
"Sounds like you're ready for a good night's sleep, Sun," says Baba Pink.

"Oh ho ho, yes I am!" Sun says. "Goodnight."

"Night, night Sun," says Baba Pink.
She kisses him goodnight.
Sun lies down on his cloud and drifts off to sleep.

Pinkhorsey is tired too.
Baba Pink strokes her soft nose.
"Just Little Star to see, then home to bed," says Baba Pink.

Little Star is twinkling in the dusky sky.
Baba Pink and Pinkhorsey fly up to see him.

"Hello, Little Star," says Baba Pink. "Are you ready to twinkle?"

Little Star can't wait to twinkle!
He waves to Baba Pink as she goes home to bed.

"Nighty night, Little Star," Baba Pink says.
"Nighty night, Baba Pink!" calls Little Star.

Inside the Cloudyhouse, the Cloudbabies and Bobo White are cosy and warm. They are snuggling up for the night.

"Goodnight, Bobo," says Baba Pink. "Goodnight Cloudbabies", says Bobo White. Baba Pink turns off her bedside light. Soon, all the Cloudbabies are fast asleep.

But then Baba Blue starts to snore! Baba Pink sits up. "Baba Blue!" she whispers. "You're snoring!" Baba Blue snorts and wakes up.

"Try lying on your side," says Baba Pink "Sorry, Baba Pink," says Baba Blue. He turns on his side and goes straight back to sleep.

High in the night sky, Little Star is shining
brightly and singing his special song.

"Twinkle twinkle
all night long.
Twinkle till the
morning comes.
Twinkle twinkle
all night long.
Twinkle till the
morning comes.
Twinkle twinkle
all night...".

RUMBLE!
RUMBLE!
RUMBLE!

Little Star stops singing. What is that loud noise?
The noise stops too, so Little Star starts singing again.

RUMBLE!
RUMBLE!
RUMBLE!

"Ooooooh," says Little Star.
"What's that funny noise? Don't like it!"

RUMBLE!
RUMBLE!
RUMBLE!

"Ooooooh!" squeals Little Star.
He zooms over to the Cloudyhouse as fast as he can.

TAPPITY TAP!
Little Star taps urgently on the glass
to wake up the Cloudbabies.
"Wakey wakey Cloudbabies!" he calls.
"Let me in!"

The Cloudbabies open their sleepy eyes.
Baba Pink gets up and opens the window. Little Star rushes inside.
"Little Star, what's wrong?" asks Baba Pink.

"Big rumbly grumble noise in the sky and I don't like it!" Little Star whimpers.

"I can't hear anything," says Baba Blue. "Can you?"
The other Cloudbabies shake their heads.
"Well Little Star's not twinkling," says Little Star. "I want to stay here, with you!"
He dives under the sheets of Baba Pink's bed.

Baba Pink sighs.
"All right, Little Star," she says.
"You can stay. But just for tonight."

The Cloudbabies settle down and Baba Pink climbs into bed. But with Little Star in her bed, she can't get comfortable. "Your points are really pointy, Little Star!" she says. "I have to get up early tomorrow to give Sun his polish. Why don't you sleep in Baba Blue's bed?"

"OK," says Little Star.

He climbs out of bed and gets in beside Baba Blue.
"Ow!" says Baba Blue. "Little Star, I have to get up early to feed the Skyhorsies tomorrow. How about sleeping in Baba Yellow's bed?"

Poor Little Star has to get up again.
"OK," he says. "Sorry!"
Little Star climbs into bed next to Baba Yellow.

"Ooooh!" says Baba Yellow. "Little Star, I have to get up early to give Rainbow's stripes a fresh coat of paint. Do you mind sleeping in Baba Green's bed?" "OK," says Little Star.

He hops over to Baba Green's bed.
This time he slides under the covers as quietly as he can.

"Little Star must be careful with pointy points," he whispers.

Baba Green doesn't wake up. "Phew," whispers Little Star. In a few seconds he is fast asleep. But then . . .

RUMBLE!
RUMBLE!
RUMBLE!

The Cloudbabies and
Little Star sit up.

"What was that?" asks Baba Blue.

**RUMBLE!
RUMBLE!
RUMBLE!**

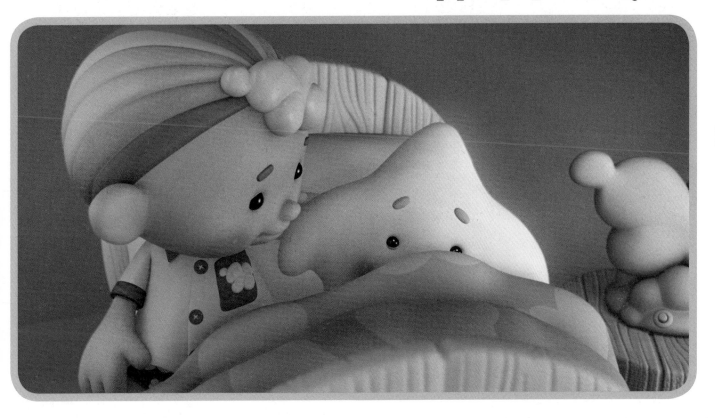

"It's the rumbly grumble noise I told you about!"
says Little Star.

Baba Pink gets up and goes to the window.
The noise is even louder now.

Little Star hides under the blankets and trembles.
"Don't like it!" he cries.

"I wonder what it is," says Baba Blue.

Baba Green looks out of the window.
"Maybe it's the clouds," he says.

Baba Blue decides to do something about it.

"Come on," he says. "We have to find out,
or none of us will get any sleep."

The Cloudbabies ride through the night sky on their Skyhorsies.
Baba Blue uses his skytorch to light up the way.

RUMBLE!
RUMBLE!
RUMBLE!

The noise is louder than ever. Little Star jumps. Baba Blue waves his torch around and lights up a big cloud.

"The noise is coming from up there," he says. "Come on."

The Cloudbabies fly up to the cloud.

RUMBLE!
RUMBLE!
RUMBLE!

The noise is so loud that it makes the cloud shake.
"What can it be?" Baba Pink wonders.
The Cloudbabies peer over the edge of the cloud. Then they start to laugh.

"So that's what's making the noise!" says Baba Pink.
"What?" asks Little Star.
"What is it?"

"It's Sun!" said the Cloudbabies
Little Star giggles. Sun is snoring!
"He's making a big noise." says Little Star.
"A big snoring noise!" says Baba Yellow.
"We'll never get to sleep with that noise,"
says Baba Blue.

"What can we do?" Baba Green asks.
Baba Pink has an idea.
"Maybe Sun is snoring because he's sleeping on his back," she says. "Like you do, Baba Blue."

Baba Blue blushes and Baba Pink smiles at him.
"But it's OK because when you turn on your side, you stop," she adds.

"I see!" says Baba Blue in an excited voice. "We should turn Sun on his side! Good idea, Baba Pink."

The Cloudbabies hop off their Skyhorsies and tiptoe over to Sun.
"Ready, Cloudbabies?" whispers Baba Blue. "One, two, three . . . push!"

They roll Sun over onto his side. The snoring stops straight away.

"It worked!" Baba Blue whispers. Little Star is amazed.
"You Cloudbabies are sooooo clever!" he says.

"Thank you Little Star," says Baba Pink. "Will you go back to twinkling now?"
"Ooooh yes!" Little Star replies. "Little Star will twinkle all night long now."

The Cloudbabies climb onto
their Skyhorsies.
Little Star is twinkling and
Sun is sleeping.
It's time for the Cloudbabies
to go home.

At the Cloudyhouse, everything
is quiet and peaceful.
All the Cloudbabies are
fast asleep in their beds.
It's going to be the best night's
sleep ever.

All About Autumn

Autumn is the third season of the year. It is cooler than summer and the days are shorter. Some trees lose their leaves in autumn.

Why do leaves change colour?

🍂 Leaves use sunshine to help them make a special kind of food for the trees.

🍂 The part of the leaf that makes the food is green. While the green part is working hard, the leaf looks green.

🍂 When the weather gets colder and there is less sunshine, the leaves stop making the special food.

🍂 Now that the green part of the leaf isn't working so hard, the other colours can show through.

That's why leaves change colour!

Signs of Autumn

🍂 The weather is windy and chilly.

🍂 Leaves turn red, yellow and orange.

🍂 You can see frost on the grass in the morning.

🍂 Animals gather food ready for the winter.

Baba Blue's Leaf Rubbing

make & do

You will need

- Crayons
- Paper
- Leaves

Keep a record of your favourite leaves with Baba Blue.

1 Collect some leaves that have fallen off the trees.

2 Put a leaf under a piece of paper, with the bumpy side facing upwards.

3 Use one hand to hold the paper still. With the other hand, rub over the paper with the side of your crayon.

4 A picture of the leaf will appear on the paper!

5 Use lots of different leaves and crayons to make a colourful autumn picture.

Autumn Fun

- Make a scrapbook of your favourite fallen leaves.

- On a windy day, go outside and fly a kite.

- Collect conkers and paint them.

Ready for Fun?

Baba Yellow has been
painting pictures of Yellowhorsey.
Look carefully at them all.
Can you spot the odd one out?

Sky Words

Baba Yellow is painting

Rainbow

Baba Pink is polishing

Sun.

Baba Blue is dusting

Moon.

Baba Green
is chasing a

cloud.

Bobo White is learning to
write. Can you help him?
Say the words and copy over
the letters with a pencil.

Fuffa's Make and Do

You will need

- Pink fabric
- Scissors
- Pen
- Hole Punch
- Fabric glue
- Paintbrush
- Cotton wool
- Blue ribbon
- Pink ribbon
  Newspaper

⚠️ Always ask a grown-up to help you when using glue, scissors and the hole punch.

🍃 Hold Fuffa up and run around to see how she moves in the wind.

🍃 What else moves in the wind?

Did you know that wind moves the clouds through the sky? Make this hanging Fuffa to show how she moves on a blowy day.

1 Fold your fabric in half and draw the picture of Fuffa Cloud onto one side.

2 Ask your grown-up to cut out the Fuffa shape. (You will have two Fuffa shapes that look exactly the same.)

3 Keep the Fuffa shapes together. Ask your grown-up to help you make some holes with the hole punch. There should be three holes along the bottom edge of the shapes and one hole at the top. (The holes will end up in the same place on each shape.)

4 Use a paintbrush to carefully paint glue around the edge of one of the shapes.

5 Place a big handful of cotton wool in the middle of the glued shape. Then put the other cloud shape on top and press down on the edges to glue the shapes together.

6 Place it on a piece of newspaper and wait for the glue to dry.

7 Push a long piece of blue ribbon through each of the bottom three holes. Tie them in place with a knot.

8 Push a pink ribbon through the top hole and tie it in place with a knot.

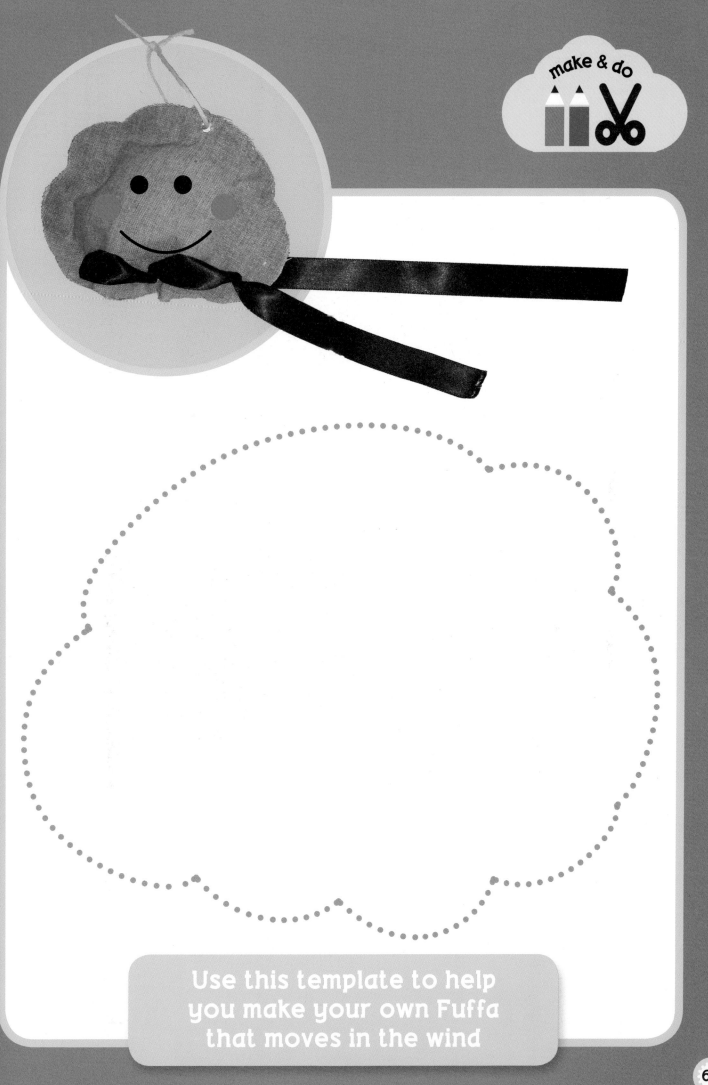

Use this template to help
you make your own Fuffa
that moves in the wind

Which Cloudbaby has collected the most Rainpears? Count them and find out.

Memory Game

Look at this picture while you count to ten three times.

Try to remember everything you can see. Then cover the picture up with a piece of paper and answer the questions.

1. Which Cloudbaby is not in the picture?
2. Who is holding a feather duster?
3. Where is Little Star?
4. What is Baba Blue holding?
5. Which Skyhorsey is in the picture?
6. Who is holding a watering can?

What else can you remember about the picture?

Did You Know...?

In autumn, the wind blows harder and the weather gets colder.

- Wind can lift things and move them around. Have you ever seen fallen leaves blowing around in the wind?

- Strong winds are called hurricanes. They can lift up heavy objects like cars!

- Wind farms use the power of wind to make electricity.

What is Wind?

- Wind is moving air. You can't see it, but you can feel it.

- The sun doesn't just warm the Earth. It warms the air too!

- Warm air is lighter than cool air, and it rises up.

- Cool air moves in to replace the warm air. This moving air is the wind!

Make a Windsock

You will need

- Toilet paper cardboard tube
- Brightly coloured ribbons
- Paint
- Paintbrush
- String
- Hole punch
- Glue
- A grown-up to help you

To find out which way the wind is blowing, you can make your very own windsock.

1 Paint the inside and outside of the cardboard tube in your favourite colour and let it dry.

2 Ask your grown-up to help you punch a hole near one end of the tube.

3 Push the string through the hole and tie it.

4 Glue the ribbons to the inside of the other end of the tube.

5 Hang up your windsock outside with the string and wait for a gust of wind to come along. The ribbons will show you which way the wind is blowing!

Snowbaby

High in the sky, up, up, in the clouds ...

It's very, very cold.
A snow cloud has covered
everything in snow.

The Cloudbabies are all wrapped up warm in their winter woollies.

Bobo White loves the snow. "Come on, Bobo," says Baba Green. "Let's go and play!" Bobo White jumps into his little sledge, and Baba Green pulls him along.

"Faster!" shouts Bobo White. "Faster, Greenybabs!"
"I love snowy days!" says Baba Yellow.
"Me too!" says Baba Pink with a giggle.

"Let's make a snowbaby!" says Baba Blue.

Baba Yellow and Baba Pink roll balls
of snow to make the head and body.

A stick for a mouth!

Buttons for eyes!   Stars for buttons!

At last it is finished.
"Our snowbaby looks great!" says Baba Pink.

Bobo White knows exactly what to call it.
"Snowybabs!" he says. "Bobo loves Snowybabs!"
He gives Snowybabs a big cuddle.

The Cloudbabies have to get on with their jobs. But Bobo White decides to stay with Snowybabs.

The Cloudbabies tell Skydonk that Bobo White isn't coming today.
Poor Skydonk looks very lonely.

Skydonk goes to find his friend. But Bobo White is singing to Snowybabs.
He is too busy to notice Skydonk.

The Cloudbabies keep popping back to check on Bobo White. "Bobo, would you and Skydonk like to help me fix the paintwell?" asks Baba Blue.

Skydonk wants to go with Baba Blue.
But Bobo White shakes his head.
"Bobo play with Snowybabs," he says.

"We're going to shake the snow off the rainpear trees," says Baba Green. "Do you want to come with us?"

Skydonk thinks that sounds like fun! But Bobo White isn't interested.
"Bobo stay here," he says.

"Would you like to help me paint Rainbow's yellow stripe?" asks Baba Yellow.
Bobo White snuggles up to Snowybabs.
"Bobo stay with Snowybabs," he says.

Bobo, why don't you and Skydonk come and help me polish Sun?" asks Baba Pink. Bobo White looks very excited. "Bobo polish Sun!" he says.

Bobo White climbs onto Skydonk, but he looks back at Snowybabs.

When Skydonk tries to fly away, Bobo White changes his mind.

"Bobo stay here," he says. Poor Skydonk looks very sad.

Baba Pink comes to take Bobo White for his nap. But he is already fast asleep. Baba Pink wraps him up nice and warm. "Look after him, Skydonk!" she says.

Baba Pink finishes polishing Sun.
"Ready for the midday shine!" she says.
"Ho ho, thanks Baba Pink," says Sun. "I'm hot,
hot, hot for a cold, cold day!"

At the paintwell, Baba Blue is starting to get hot. All the icicles are dripping and melting. "Phew!" says Baba Blue. "Sun is shining brightly today!"

Baba Green is shaking the snow off the rainpear trees. "It's melting quickly," he says. "The snow will be gone soon."

Bobo White wakes up, stretches and gives a big yawn. Then he looks for Snowybabs but he has melted away.

"Snowybabs?" he cries.
"SNOWYBABS!"
Poor Bobo White!

Skydonk tries to tell Bobo White what has happened. But Bobo White doesn't understand. He wants to go and look for Snowybabs.

Just then, Baba Pink arrives on Pinkhorsey.
"Snowybabs gone!" wails Bobo White.

"Snowybabs hasn't gone anywhere," says Baba Pink. "It's just melted."

Bobo White still doesn't understand. So Baba Pink holds up a lump of snow.

When Sun shines on it, the snow melts away.

"No!" Bobo cries. "Naughty melty Sun!" He frowns at Sun. "I can't help it," says Sun. "I'm hot, hot, hot!"

"Sun can't help shining, Bobo," says Baba Pink.
"But don't worry. When it snows,
we can make Snowybabs again."

Bobo White jumps up and down.
"More snow!" he demands.
"Snow now!"
"The snow cloud's gone, Bobo,"
says Baba Pink.
Bobo White is very upset.

"The snow cloud must be up
here somewhere,"
says Sun in a friendly voice.
"Why don't we look for it?"
"Good idea, Sun!" says Baba Pink.
"Why don't we all go and look
for the snow cloud in the
Skytrain?"

The Cloudbabies and Bobo White wait on the platform. Baba Pink rings the bell. Then the clouds join together and turn into the Skytrain! "Ready everyone?" asks Baba Blue. "Let's find the snow cloud!"

Everyone climbs aboard. WHOOSH!
The Skytrain zooms up into the sky.
Skydonk is fast asleep. Overhead, the snow cloud appears and starts to snow again.

It covers Skydonk up!

The Cloudbabies search the sky for the snow cloud, but it is nowhere to be seen.

They all hop out at the station. "It's no good," says Baba Pink. "I think the snow cloud's gone away."

Bobo White is very sad. But then he spots something above the garden.
"Snow cloud!" he shouts.

Skydonk is still asleep under the snow.
Bobo White spots the white Skydonk shape.

"Snowdonk!" says Bobo White.
"Wow!" says Baba Pink. "The snow cloud has
made a snowdonk just for you, Bobo."
"Let's show the snowdonk to Skydonk," says
Baba Green. "He'll love it!"

"DONK!" calls Bobo White. But Skydonk doesn't come. "SKYDONK!" shout the Cloudbabies.

"Donk gone," sniffs Bobo White. "No more Donk. Bobo love Donk!" Suddenly, the snowdonk yawns and stretches.

He shakes the snow off. It's Skydonk!

"Snowdonk was Skydonk all along!" says Baba Green. Bobo White gives Skydonk a big hug, and Skydonk nuzzles him.
"Bobo loves Skydonk!"

All About Winter

Winter is the last season of the year. It is the coldest season and it can bring snow and hail. Lots of wild animals have trouble finding food in winter.

Winter is Baba Pink's favourite time of year!

Why Do We Have Seasons?

We have different seasons because the Earth spins around the sun. It takes Earth one year to go around the sun. As the place where you live turns closer to the sun, the weather changes and gets warmer.

Signs of Winter

* Some wild animals snuggle down to sleep for the whole season. This is called hibernating.

* You wear coats, hats, gloves and scarves to keep warm.

* The cold weather makes spiders' webs frosted and sparkling.

* Families are kept warm with radiators and heaters.

Baba Pink's Sparkley Pinecones

You will need

- Pinecones
- Glue
  Paintbrush
- Silver glitter
- A large plastic freezer bag
- Sheets of newspaper

⚠️ Always ask a grown-up to help you when using plastic bags and glue.

Collect pinecones on a winter walk and make these pretty decorations with Baba Pink.

1 Ask your grown-up to help you make a mixture of two parts glue and one part water.

2 Use a large paintbrush to coat the pinecones in the glue mixture.

3 Put some glitter into the freezer bag and then add the gluey pinecones.

4 Seal the freezer bag and shake well!

5 Open the bag and take out the pinecones. Shake any extra glitter onto sheets of newspaper.

Winter Fun

✳ Go sledging in the snow and look for animal tracks.

✳ Put food and water out for the birds and watch them with binoculars.

✳ Make a snowbaby in the snow.

Ready for Fun?

Sky Friends

The Cloudbabies have forgotten to dust, polish and paint their Sky Friends. Use your crayons to make Sun, Moon, Rainbow, Little Star and Fuffa Cloud bright and colourful again.

Star Eve Bunting

make & do

These beautiful stars will watch over you and twinkle all night long.

You will need

- Pieces of card
- Pencil
- Scissors
- Gold pen
- Glitter
- Glue
- Hole punch
- Ribbon

 Always ask a grown-up to help you when using scissors.

1 Copy this star template onto some card ten times.

2 Ask your grown-up to cut out the star shapes.

3 Use your gold pen and glitter to make the stars sparkle.

4 Make a hole in the top of each star with the hole punch.

5 String the stars onto the ribbon and hang them across your window.

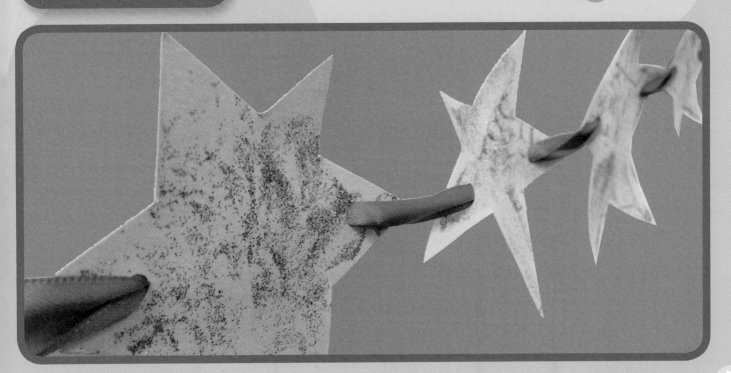

Did You Know...?

In winter, the nights are longer and there is more time to snuggle up in bed. Do you love night-time as much as the Cloudbabies?

⭐ There are billions of stars in the sky.

⭐ Some stars are older than others.

⭐ Stars come in different sizes. Some of them are very small, just like Little Star.

⭐ Some stars are arranged in patterns that look like animals or objects. Ask a grown-up to show you one!

What is night?

⭐ The Earth spins around the sun.

⭐ When the place where you live is pointing away from the sun, it is night-time.

What is a star?

⭐ A star is a ball made of hot, glowing gas.

⭐ Stars can shine for millions or even billions of years.

⭐ The stars you can see in the sky are very, very far away.

What is the moon?

⭐ The moon is made of rock, and it spins around the Earth.

⭐ It is the brightest thing in the night sky.

Twinkle stars,

Twinkling so bright

On this special night.

You'll make our star-eve look lovely and bright.

Glittering,

Shimmering,

Distantly glimmering.

You will make everything glow with delight

On our special night.

Sing this sleepy lullaby with Little Star.

Night Night!

Who is Baba Yellow tucking up in bed? Join the dots to find out and then colour in the picture.

Hungry Horsies

The Skyhorsies are enjoying some horseyhay. Colour them in as they munch!

Night Sky Star Biscuits

make & do

You will need

- 4ozs soft margerine
- 3 ozs butter
- 2 ozs icing sugar
- 5 ozs plain flour
- 4 ozs self raising flour
- 1 tablespoon cornflour
- Star-shaped biscuit cutter (optional)

⚠️ Ask a grown-up to help you when using the oven.

Follow these steps to make your own tasty version of the night sky!

1 Beat margerine and butter together, until soft.

2 Gradually beat in the sifted icing sugar until light and fluffy.

3 Work in the two sifted flours and cornflower to make a smooth, soft dough.

4 Wrap in foil and chill for 30 mins.

5 Heat the oven to Gas Mark 4/180°C/350F.

6 Roll out the pastry to 6mm (1/4") thick on floured surface. The dough will be very soft.

7 Either cut out with a star shaped cookie cutter or hand form into the shape of a star.

8 Place on a greased baking tray and cook for about 10 mins, or until light brown.

9 Allow to cool and decorate with icing and cake decorations.

10 To decorate:
Make up white glace icing (just icing sugar and water) and colour half the mixture with yellow edible food colouring. The icing should be runny enough to drop off the back of a spoon.

Ready for Fun?

Can you colour in this picture of the Star Tree?

Starry Night

It's nighting time and the Cloudbabies are going to bed.

How many stars can you count in the sky?

Answers

Page 23

Page 24

Page 44

Page 45

Page 62

Page 66
Baba Green has the most rainpears.

Page 67
1. Baba Yellow
2. Baba Pink
3. At the window
4. Toolbox
5. Pinkhorsey
6. Baba Green

Page 92
There are 8 stars